Where The
Blood Runs Thin

Paige Damerau

Dedication

I dedicate this book to my fiancée, the love of my life, Abigail
Dorantes, as well as to my family and friends.

Acknowledgment

I would like to thank Keith Eckermann for his guidance and encouragement throughout the completion of this book.

Special thanks to Mathew Baker for his input and editing, and to Bill Jordan for his contributions.

I'm also grateful to Christopher Cody Jordan for his ideas and help with visualization.

Most of all, I thank my fiancée, Abigail Dorantes, for her unwavering support.

About the Author

Paige Damerau was born in Luling, Texas, and raised in the small town of Moulton, Texas. A graduate of Moulton High School, Paige has always had a deep interest in history. When researching the past, Paige enjoys visualizing life in that era and imagining what it would have been like to live during those times.

Contents

Chapter 1: The Hunt

1861

I walk with Sarah Rogers.

"I love you, Sarah, but I need to fight in the war. I wouldn't be mad if you found someone new. I know we've been courting for two years, but I have to fight for what we believe in."

Sarah looks at me with tears in her eyes. "Just be safe, please," she says as the rain falls on their heads, dripping from the leaves of the old oak tree on the ranch. The sky is grey, the grass stands tall, and the quarter horses are soaked. The buckboard wagon is covered and drenched.

I kiss Sarah one last time, then look into her eyes. "Goodbye, Sarah," I whisper before riding away.

Paige!

I awoke to someone shouting, "Paige! Paige, get up!"

"Marshal Johnson's here," Keith said as he took off my sheets, trying to get me to stand up. "Dad's takin' to him right now. We need to go n' check it out."

Fearing something bad had happened, I immediately stood up and was about to step forward when someone suddenly barged into the room. My second brother, Chris, looked between me and Keith before yelling out, "Momma's crying! Get downstairs, now!"

We all turned and ran out of the bedroom and down the flight of stairs in our home. We ran into the kitchen and found our mother, Betsy, slumped over a table, sobbing uncontrollably. My brothers and I looked at each other, wondering what we could say to try and comfort her and to figure out what was happening.

The outside door to the kitchen opened, and two men walked in—my father, Reno, and Marshal Johnson.

Johnson looked at all of our confused faces and motioned to my dad. "Well, Reno, you want to' tell them, or should I do it?"

Reno nodded at the Marshal and then took a couple of steps closer to us. He first glanced at Mom, noticing how she was still crying considerably, though it was probably much worse when Johnson first presented the news to them.

"Sons," my dad began, turning back toward us. His face looked as if he was trying to process what he was about to say. "Your three other brothers... they're in some mighty trouble right now. Matt, Cody, and Bill all just committed murder—"

We gasped.

At that point, my mother burst into tears even harder. My father ran over to her and pulled her up into an embrace. She wrapped her arms around him and buried her face into his neck, her sobs turning into wailing at this point.

There was only one other time when I saw my mom like that: the horrified look on her face—it was when the Civil War started, when Matt and I left to join the Confederacy. We were the only two brothers out of our whole family who wanted to fight for our very way of living. Mom was terrified when we left the house... and for good reason.

I remember killing one of the Union soldiers for the very first time—he was just a young kid, probably having just joined up like me and Matt. It was a terrible feeling, but after just watching the Yankees killing everyone in a nearby town—women and children included—setting fire to all the buildings and completely torching the place... I felt it was justified.

Matt and I were so fucking pissed that we decided to come up with plans to try and kill as many of them sons-of-bitches as possible. And, to an extent, we did. We would ambush the Union soldiers at every opportunity we could possibly get, counting up their casualties with each attack. Matt was especially brutal, kicking off each ambush by igniting a cannonball filled with gunpowder. It was awesome seeing those bastards getting blown up.

During bigger engagements, whenever the Union had to fall back, we would be given a unit to go around and flank their retreating forces, causing as much chaos in their ranks as possible.

After one ambush, one of the Yankees survived. We carried the fucker back to one of our spare horses and tied him to the back of the stallion's legs. Matt smacked the horse's rear end hard, forcing the creature to take off into a sprint. We saw that Union soldier get dragged across the adjacent meadow, and after about five minutes, the rope tore, and the man flew up into the air and landed with a thud.

We walked over to the body, and when we discovered he was still alive, Matt pulled out his Colt Army Model 1860 and shot him in the head—no more fucking around at that point.

These were the horrors of war that Mom knew about. She didn't want Matt and me to go because she knew what we would encounter, what we would do. Now, seeing that same look on her face reminded me of all the bad shit we had to do in order to fight the North. Though the Confederates lost anyway, we put up one hell of a fight, and we made the Union soldiers fight for every fucking square mile.

"Paige Calvary."

I snapped out of my thoughts and focused on the person calling my name—Marshal Johnson. He walked forward until he was standing right in front of me and my brothers. "I'm going to do what I can to bring these boys to justice. But, seeing as how you and Matt both served in the Confederacy, I would suggest you come along and help me track him down along with your other brothers."

Mom intervened. "Paige, please don't go!"

I saw my father adjusting his grip on her, rubbing his hands across her shoulders and back. He leaned into her ear and soothed her. "Paige can handle them, boys. He and Marshal Johnson will be alright."

"He's right, Mom," I said as I walked over to her and grasped one of her hands. "I'll be careful."

We hugged each other, and it felt like an eternity before she finally released me.

"We'd best be leaving soon," Johnson said. "Get your stuff together and meet me outside."

"Will do, Marshal," I replied.

As Johnson turned and walked outside, I said goodbye to my father and my two other brothers. I went back upstairs and grabbed my gear and weapons. After straightening out all my ammunition and other necessities, I holstered my .44 caliber Colt Dragoon revolver and then grabbed my 1874-pattern Sharps rifle. I looked it over, and then the realization of what possibly happened finally hit me...

I might have to kill my own brothers...

I grabbed my horse and threw the saddle up onto its back. The Marshal was already on his own horse, waiting for me further down the path leading to my family's home. I climbed up and looked back toward the house. My parents and brothers were watching me, fear and concern plastered on all of their faces, my mom especially—her eyes were still shedding tears.

I gave them a subtle nod, a possible final goodbye, before turning and heading in the Marshal's direction.

"Paige, wait!"

I turned around, and Keith stepped forward.

"What are you doing?" I asked, slightly annoyed. I didn't want to get anyone else involved and risk their lives in what might end up devolving into a brutal firefight where none of us would make it back.

"I'm going with you," he replied.

Now, I was definitely annoyed. "Like hell you are!"

"Listen, just hear me out," Keith gestured with his hands. "I don't believe Matt, Bill, and Cody killed that man. I just don't... especially Matt."

"Why's that?"

His brother stepped forward. "Matt was a traveler. He tried to settle down, but don't you remember when those fucking northerners went to that town and wiped out everyone and everything? He was just as pissed as you were!"

Shaking his head, he continued, "A war of attrition, that's what they said... I could maybe see Matt killing some retired soldier who fought for the Union, but there is no way he would help kill an innocent man. You two were inseparable during the war, and you know it as much as I do. There's got to be more to this story, Paige."

I looked at Keith for what felt like forever before finally muttering, "I hope you're right, Keith."

"Matt's home is here in these parts," he said, turning to look at their house. "And between the war and whatever the hell this shit is that's going on right now, he's never had a chance to realize it fully."

"Then answer me this," I said, hunching forward. "Why the fuck wouldn't Matt go down to the saloon with Bill and Cody? The three of them have been hanging out a lot lately."

Keith looked at me with a concerned expression. "Something else may have happened at the saloon. No matter what, though, we need to find them before they get killed." I met with the Marshal, who told Keith and me that he was riding to get some help.

We rode into the town of Gunbarrel and went straight to the saloon. I walked in with Keith and looked around.

"Let's ask some questions," I said.

A pretty blonde-haired woman in her late twenties approached me. "Hey, my name is Mary. What's yours?"

"Paige," I replied with a smile, thinking she was a beautiful woman. "This is my brother, Keith. We came to ask about the shooting that happened two days ago."

Mary's eyes widened. "Yes, Paige, I saw two men. Their names were Bill and Cody Calvary. They held down the old man, Mark Mason, and Matt Calvary shot him."

While I was talking to Mary, three men got up and bumped into me.

I spun around. "What's y'all's problem?"

The men looked at me and Keith with a mix of anger and guilt.

Mary glanced at me. "Don't worry about them, Paige. I'll help you find your brothers—if you pay me."

Keith turned to me. "Don't do it. I don't trust her."

I looked at Keith. "She could be helpful."

Keith sighed. "Okay, if you say so."

I got up and walked over to the saloon owner, Jerry McDonald. "What happened here that night?"

He sighed and said, "Matt, Bill, and Cody were sitting at the table in the back corner, playing poker with a gambler named

Mark Mason and a couple of rough-looking men—Jake 'Rattlesnake' Hufford, Harry 'Texas Bull,' and Andy 'Hangman Kid' Jackson."

Keith's eyes widened as realization dawned on him. "They might have framed our brothers."

I asked, "What exactly happened?"

Jerry finished his drink, his expression darkening. "All I know is that a hard storm blew in, knocked out the lights, and then a gunshot rang out. When the lights came back on, Mark Mason was lying on his stomach with a bullet in his back. Jake 'Rattlesnake' Hufford said it was Matt, Cody, and Bill."

"Where did they ride to?" I asked.

"South towards Devil's Canyon."

Me, Keith, and Mary left town, riding together. As I looked at Mary, I couldn't help but notice her beautiful blonde hair and blue eyes. Keith shot me a knowing look—he could tell I was letting a woman mess with my thinking.

I turned to Mary. "Where are you from?"

She giggled. "Arizona."

"What are you doing in Texas?" I asked.

She sighed. "Both my parents were killed by cattle rustlers. My father tried to stop them but was shot. My mother, Francine, was killed trying to get to him. My aunt and uncle took me in, and we moved here when I was just a little girl."

I looked at her with sympathy, watching the sadness in her eyes. "I know what that's like. Believe me."

Me, Keith, and Mary set up camp in an area surrounded by trees, a creek bed, and open plains with a hill and a few scattered trees.

Mary looked at me. "We don't have any food. We need to find some."

Keith, looking unsure, nodded. "Yeah, you're right."

Mary turned to me. "I'm going to pick some wild green onions."

I nodded. "Okay, that sounds good for cooking."

Mary smiled and walked away.

While the boys were distracted, hunting for food, Mary slipped away and met with Jake "Rattlesnake" Hufford, Harry "Texas Bull," and Andy "Hangman Kid" Jackson. She told them, "Paige and Keith are looking for their brothers—Matt, Cody, and Bill. They think y'all killed Mark Mason."

Jake kissed Mary on the cheek. "Thanks for telling me, love. Now keep following them."

Mary nodded in agreement.

Back at camp, Keith looked at me. "I don't trust her."

I sighed. "You don't trust anyone."

Keith spotted a deer rubbing its antlers on a tree, shedding its velvet. He raised his rifle and took the shot. The buck collapsed.

As Keith walked toward the deer, Mary appeared from the woods. Keith turned to her. "Where were you? What were you doing?"

Mary hesitated before answering. "Picking wild onions."

Keith narrowed his eyes. "I don't believe you."

Mary shrugged. "Fine, don't." She headed back to camp.

Keith turned his head and saw four men riding in the distance—the same men from the saloon.

He walked over to me. "Help me with the deer."

I followed him to where the buck had fallen. As we picked it up, Keith whispered, "Mary came from the woods, but she didn't pick anything. Those men from the saloon were there too."

I shrugged. "They're probably just passing through."

We carried the deer through the green grass and weeds as the sun began to set. When we returned to camp, Mary was cooking onions over the fire. I helped Keith skin the deer, and he cooked the meat. The fire crackled high.

As we ate, Mary glanced at me with a seductive look and whispered, "Can I talk to you in private?"

Keith watched as Mary and I disappeared into the woods. The crickets chirped, the fire crackled, frogs croaked, and the creek flowed steadily.

Deep in the woods, she turned to me. "So, what do you want to talk about?"

I leaned in and kissed her, pulling off her shirt and running my hands over her soft skin. She kissed me with passion. I kissed her neck, her shoulders, her collarbone. She slipped out of her dress, revealing her beautiful body. We lay in the thick grass. I ran my hand along her leg, and she moaned. We had sex, then fell into each other's arms.

"I love you, Mary," I whispered.

She looked at me. "I love you too."

The next morning, I woke up with Mary beside me, wrapped in my duster. She sat up, buttoned her shirt, and grabbed her hat. Gently, she woke me with a kiss. "Morning, love."

I smiled, my heart swelling. "Morning, Paige. Last night was amazing."

She smiled back. "It really was."

I gazed at her, my love for her deep and unwavering. "I love you, Paige."

She held my hand and helped me up. "I love you too." Hearing those words, I felt safe and secure with her.

The river flowed beautifully, birds chirped in the trees, and squirrels played in the branches. The sky was a bright, cloudless blue.

As we walked back to camp, we saw an old man standing in front of Keith, holding a rifle.

Keith looked at us and sighed, his expression filled with anger and disappointment. "I'm glad you two finally showed up." His eyes locked onto mine, his face saying, *Paige, if you had been here, I wouldn't have been held up.*

I shot him a look that said, *My apologies.*

Stepping forward, I addressed the old man. "What do you want?"

The man narrowed his eyes and pointed his rifle at me. "You're on my land," he said angrily.

I met his gaze, keeping my voice calm. "We're just passing through. We're looking for three men who murdered someone in town."

The old man studied me, then replied, "That's it? You just spent the night here?"

He paused before adding, "You need a scout? I was a scout in the war."

I raised an eyebrow. "Really?"

"Whose side?" the old man asked.

I looked at him. "Yankee side."

He nodded. "Well, I'm a Johnny Reb, but if you are who you say you are, I could use the help."

I studied the old man. "My name is Paige Calvery. This is my brother, Keith, and this is Mary."

The old man lowered his gun. "I'm Timothy William."

"I'll pay you money if we find the men," I said.

Mary looked at me with concern. I paused, sighed, and looked back at her.

"Can you even trust this man?" she asked.

Keith interrupted. "What's wrong? Afraid? Afraid of a pay cut?"

Mary shot Keith a glare. "No, I'm in love with Paige, Keith. And he loves me. So, stop being insecure."

I looked between Mary and Keith before nodding at Timothy. "Let's go, Mr. Williams."

We packed up camp, gathered our gear, and followed Timothy through the prairie on horseback. As we rode, I watched Mary's hair blow in the wind, admiring her beauty. The tall grass swayed in waves, bluebonnets were blooming, and the wind howled across the open land.

Timothy looked back at us. "We're going through Comanche country, so watch out. Keep your eyes peeled."

I rolled a cigarette, struck a match against my chaps, took a drag, and exhaled slowly, feeling a slight buzz.

Timothy glanced at Keith. "I don't trust Mary."

Keith scoffed. "Tell me about it," he muttered, his face darkening.

Up on the hill, hidden among the trees, Jake—aka Rattlesnake Hufford—watched us alongside his men: Harry—aka Texas Bull—and Andy—aka Hangman Kid Jackson.

Jake smirked. "Follow them."

Harry and Andy chuckled.

Andy spoke in a menacing tone. "Yeah, let's follow them. I'm itching to kill."

We continued through a rocky canyon when Timothy suddenly looked up and spotted two men with guns on the cliffs above us.

"Let's move it! Quick!" he yelled.

I kicked my horse's sides, urging it forward, letting Mary and Keith go ahead of me. Mary glanced back at me, concern in her eyes.

I gave her a calm look and said gently, "Keep moving. Don't worry about me."

Keith nodded. "Keep her safe," I told him.

They rode ahead while I turned my horse around, letting the men follow me. I raced out of the canyon, dirt and rocks kicking up beneath my horse's hooves. The tall grass blurred past me as I galloped across the prairie. I looked back—two masked men were gaining on me. Bandits.

I pulled my rifle from its sheath and aimed.

Meanwhile, Mary looked at Keith and Timothy, worry on her face. "Should we help him?"

Keith clenched his jaw. "He can handle it. Now move it!"

Mary's eyes filled with fear as gunshots echoed behind us, but she followed Keith and Timothy on horseback.

I kept riding, the men closing in. I reached an oak tree, jumped off my horse, and took cover. Gunfire erupted. Bullets ricocheted off the tree, dirt flying everywhere. One of the men cursed.

"Get 'em, Jimmy!" one yelled.

"I can't hit shit!" another yelled.

"Keep trying, Sid!"

I spotted a boulder by a tree and ran for it. Sid and Jimmy—those were their names—walked closer, guns raised.

I fired first. Two shots. One to each chest.

They dropped.

I ran to my horse, mounted up, and took off. That's when I spotted a strange woman in the distance, riding with someone. She looked familiar, but the sun was too bright, burning my eyes. She was heading my way, fast. But I didn't have time to wait.

I turned my horse and rode back through the canyons, pushing hard to catch up with Mary, Keith, and Timothy. It took a day and a half, but I finally found them camped at an abandoned Pony Express outpost. The place had a corral, a bunkhouse, and an office with a bed, a stove, and a fireplace.

I arrived just in time to hear Mary yelling.

"We have to go back for him, Keith!"

"It's too dangerous!" Keith shot back.

Mary's voice trembled. "He's your brother! And he's my love!"

Keith clenched his fists. "I know! But Paige can handle himself!"

Timothy cursed. "Goddammit, we aren't going to look for him, Mary!"

***

Meanwhile, miles away, Marshal Johnson and Sarah set up camp.

Sarah looked at him. "We need to find Paige and Keith before Jake, Harry, and Andy do."

Marshal Johnson nodded. "I know. Matt, Cody, and Bill didn't shoot the gambler. After Jake blew out the candle, Mark Mason was shot—and Andy blamed them."

Sarah sighed and lay down by the fire. "I'm worried about the Calvery brothers. Especially Paige."

Marshal Johnson gave her a knowing look. "I know. But all we can do is find them and warn them."

He draped a blanket over her as she drifted off to sleep.

Chapter 2: Unaware of the Storm

I walked into the back where Mary, Keith, and Timothy were standing. They didn't notice me at first, so I watched them for a moment. Then Mary turned her head, and before I could say anything, she jumped on me, kissing me.

"You're alive! I was worried about you!"

"I told you I'd be okay, Mary," I said, hugging her tightly. She laid her head on my chest, her long blonde hair blowing in the wind as the sun began to set.

Timothy and Keith came up when they heard the commotion. They patted my shoulders.

"Knew you'd make it," Keith said matter-of-factly.

"You're one strong lad," Timothy added.

Timothy and Keith went inside to cook a squirrel and rabbit stew in the big kettle pot. Mary and I stayed outside, peeling potatoes that had been grown in the garden. She had picked them up before I arrived. We added the potatoes to the pot for Keith and Timothy, and Mary chopped up wild onions from the garden, tossing them in.

The smell of the stew was good, but the fire made me feel hot, so I stepped outside. I heard coyotes and crickets in the distance. The horses in the corral made noises. I rolled a cigarette, struck a match on my chaps, and took a slow puff, looking up at the sky. Lightning bolts reflected in the clouds.

"Dinner's ready," Mary called.

I went inside and sat next to Mary while Keith and Timothy sat across from us. Keith gave me a look and then glanced at Mary, shaking his head. He still didn't trust her. We ate dinner quietly. When we were done, I turned to Keith.

"If you want, you can clean, and I'll check the horses in the corral."

Keith nodded and started washing. Timothy helped him, using ash from the fire in the wood-burning stove to scrub the dishes. Mary fetched water from the outside faucet, hand-cranking it.

As she filled the bucket, I saw her glance off into the distance. A moment later, she rushed back to Keith and Timothy, setting the bucket down.

"I'll be back," she said in a hurry.

Keith and Timothy shook their heads. Meanwhile, I was in the corral, feeding and watering the horses, completely unaware of any danger.

Not far from us, Jake, Harry, and Andy were camped out, waiting.

"She'll come," Harry said.

Back at the bunkhouse, Keith, Timothy, and I fell asleep, unaware that Mary had sneaked off to see Jake.

When she reached him, he grinned. "Hey, sweetie, what you got?" he asked, kissing her.

"They're headed to Killer's Canyon," she told him.

Lightning flashed, and thunder roared. She continued speaking to Jake, Harry, and Andy.

"I'm telling you guys, that's where Keith thinks his brothers are."

She hid her feelings for me, and Jake kissed her again.

"Go back, babe, 'cause we don't want them suspicious," Jake said.

Mary nodded, but I wasn't there to see the regret on her face.

By the time she sneaked back into the bunkhouse and crawled into bed beside me, I was deep in a dream.

I dream of Sarah, the beautiful dark-haired woman with blue eyes I left behind for the war. I see her sweet smile and the kindness on her face as she sits on a wagon at the ranch. I walk up to her and smile back. But something is different. Her body trembles with fear, and her eyes fill with tears.

With a cracked voice, she says, "Paige, I missed you, but you gotta go."

Then, in the dream, a flash of lightning strikes, and a flood washes over us, sweeping us both away.

I woke up with a start. The storm outside had worsened—thunder cracked, lightning flashed, and heavy rain turned the ground to mud. Water flooded the low spots.

"Paige, we need to get moving. There are four men on horseback riding this way," Keith said.

I looked at him. "How do you know?"

"Timothy told me. He went out to check the horses and saw them."

Mary rushed over, bringing me my horse. I met her gaze, feeling a sense of love and safety. I helped her onto her horse and mounted mine. Timothy climbed onto his own, and he looked at us.

"Follow me," he said.

We rode behind Timothy, the night wind chilling me to the bone. The scent of rain grew stronger. Thunder roared, lightning flashed, and the downpour made it nearly impossible to see. Timothy struck a match and lit his lantern.

"There, see it?" he said, pointing ahead.

He was pointing at a valley where a cabin sat, surrounded by trees and rocks.

Timothy looked at me and Keith. "Let's go check it out."

We made our way toward the cabin. As we got closer, I saw the glow of candlelight inside. Mary shivered beside me. I pulled off my duster and handed it to her.

"Get on with my horse," I told her, helping her up so she could ride with me.

She wrapped her arms around me as I leaned over to grab the reins of her horse. We carefully rode down a muddy slope.

I turned to the others. "We need to get off these horses and walk them. The mud is thick, and the rain is coming down too damn hard now."

A bolt of lightning lit up the ground, revealing just how dangerous the path was. Keith and Timothy dismounted, and we led the horses through the valley.

Suddenly, from the cabin, a voice shouted, "Stop! Who goes there?"

I recognized Matt's voice. Then I saw Bill and Cody standing beside him, their guns pointed at us.

I called back, "Matt! Bill! Cody! It's me, your brother, Paige! I got Keith, Mary, and Timothy with me!"

"Mary?" Bill yelled.

"Let them in," Matt said.

We stepped inside, the warmth of the cabin hitting me instantly. Mary looked uneasy as if she were carrying some kind of guilt.

Before she could slip away, Keith blocked her path. "Where are you going?"

"Let me go," she said.

I met Keith's eyes and spoke firmly. "Let her go."

Matt spoke up. "Bill and Cody, doesn't she look like the girl who accused us at the saloon? The one that was all over the gambler?"

Timothy realized they were onto something and looked at Keith and me. "Maybe your brothers are innocent. Mary here has been sneaking out more than usual. Think about it—she left last night while we were busy doing chores and came back while we were sleeping."

I noticed the shift in the room. Mary knew Timothy, Keith, Cody, and Bill had caught on. I wanted to believe she had just gone for a night walk or stepped out for air, but deep down, I felt she was fooling me. My stomach twisted with doubt. I should have admitted my suspicions, but instead, I said, "Maybe she went for a walk and got fresh air."

Keith yelled in annoyance. "Come on, Paige! I saw those men from the saloon following when we set up camp by the creek. Remember when Mary came back with no onions?"

Matt, Cody, Bill, and Timothy all looked at me, waiting for my response. They knew I wasn't taking Keith's side.

"Like I said before, they could be drifters or just people riding," Keith explained.

Mary played innocent, hiding whatever guilt she had. "I just saw what I saw at the saloon, and I didn't wander off to meet up with no one. I was just wandering to get fresh air and find wild onions."

She stood beside me, her eyes pleading, a clear sign she wanted me to believe her. "You believe Paige, don't you?"

I nodded. "Yes."

I glanced at Keith, Matt, Bill, Cody, and Timothy.

Bill scoffed and yelled, "He is whooped! So far, she'll tell him to kill one of us, and he'll do it!"

I shot Bill a glare. From the corner of my eye, I caught Mary smirking when no one was looking.

The tension in the room finally settled. Cody pulled out a cotton sack and revealed a black powder 5 shot cap and ball of 32 caliber. It was broken—the hammer didn't go all the way up.

Bill looked at Cody. "I thought you would get rid of that damn thing."

Cody shrugged. "Well, before the saloon ordeal, I wanted to take it to the gunsmith but forgot about it. It shoots if I hit the hammer."

Bill, Matt, and Keith exchanged looks before laughing.

Timothy started cooking—beans, cured bacon, and eggs that Matt had picked up when we stocked up at the general store before heading to the saloon. The cabin fell quiet. The storm had finally passed. I stepped outside, smoking a cigarette and watching the moon and clouds drift across the sky. Behind the cabin, the horses were tied to the post. I could hear them making noises.

Mary came outside and wrapped her arms around me. I took a slow drag of my cigarette, inhaling and exhaling. We stayed quiet.

Suddenly, Mary's body tensed. Her eyes widened as she spotted Jake, Harry, and Andy—along with more riders. In a rush, she grabbed me and yanked me inside.

I frowned. "What was that for?"

She looked at me. "Dinner."

Right on cue, Timothy called out, "Dinner is ready."

I sat next to Mary. Keith sat beside Timothy while Cody and Bill took their usual spots.

Cody spoke up. "Before we eat, let's say grace."

I glanced at Matt. He and I had never said grace during the war. Bill and Keith both looked at us.

"One blessing won't hurt since y'all two always left the table when Mom said prayer," Cody said.

Cody led the prayer. We all said, "Amen," and then we ate.

Mary turned to Matt. "So, you and Paige were in the Civil War?"

I stiffened and cut her off. "We don't talk about it."

Matt's expression hardened. "Don't ask us."

Mary nodded, understanding. We continued eating in silence.

Bill stirred things up. "So, Matt, how does it feel to have all the brothers back together again? I mean, we wouldn't be running if you hadn't told us, 'Let's go to the saloon and drink.'"

Matt slammed his fist on the table, making everyone jump. "We may not have gotten in trouble if you would've kept your mouth shut! We wouldn't be in this position!"

Cody yelled, "Knock it off, y'all two!"

Keith jumped in, breaking up the fight, while I pulled Mary close, keeping her calm.

Then, Timothy heard something outside. He went to check and saw Jake, Harry, Andy, and their gang. Before he could react, Mary bolted out the door toward them.

I got up and followed, a sinking feeling settling in my chest. The truth hit me like a punch to the gut—Mary had played me like a fool. Hurt and betrayed, I shouted, "Mary, you betrayed us!"

She turned to me, guilt written all over her face, but before she could say a word, Jake stepped forward.

"That's what I love about Mary," he taunted. "She likes to play guys. I just want to let you know that tomorrow, you, your brothers, and that scout are going to die. I got a gang, and your brothers—they didn't kill that man. I was behind the gambler with my revolver, and when the candles died out, I had Harry and Andy hold them. Then I shot him. Mary was helping me, making that guy believe she loved him to take the money off him. And, well, your brothers were the ticket to my escape— the perfect escape. And Mary here was my little spy. She left y'all's camp so she could tell me everything."

I stood there, fists clenched, as they rode off, their laughter echoing through the night. Jake's voice rang out one last time. "You all are dead!"

Keith, Matt, Bill, and Cody were right. They had been right all along.

I turned to them, my voice laced with regret. "Damn. I'm sorry for not believing you about her."

Keith let out a sigh. "Well, hell, a woman's spell, brother."

Bill added, "Hell, that could've been any of us falling hard over a woman like that."

Matt cut through it all. "My main concern now is the fight that's about to happen."

I grabbed my 1874 Sharps rifle from the saddle and walked inside. It was time to prepare. Now that I knew the truth about my brothers, I felt like I had let them down—let my guard down for a woman and failed them. But there was no time for regret. The only thing that mattered now was fighting and keeping them safe.

Chapter 3: Jake has Friends

Mary rode with Jake, and Harry and Andy followed them to their gang. Jake helped Mary down and asked, "Did the Calvery brothers know anything about our gang of Comancheros?"

Mary looked at him and replied, "Never told them."

Jake kissed Mary passionately and whispered in her ear, "We are alone."

She felt guilty—the way Paige kissed her, the way he moved with her, treated her nice and sweet, not rough. She slept with Jake but couldn't help thinking about the first time she made love with Paige.

The Comanches rode up. Andy looked at them and spoke to the tribe leader named Running Deer. Harry looked at Running Deer and said, "If you're looking for Jake, he's in his tent with Mary."

Running Deer smirked. Harry called, "Javier, go get the whiskey and rifles."

The other Comancheros sat, drank, laughed, and messed with the women. The Comanches took the whiskey and rifles. Then one of them, named Loose Feather, rode up with others and handed the horses to the Comancheros before leaving.

As they started riding away, a Comanche scout named Sharp Eyes rode up and told Running Deer, "Lawman with a white woman coming—two miles that way."

Running Deer let out a war cry, signaling the ride.

Chapter 4: Marshal and the Angel

Marshal Johnson and Sarah stopped at the Pony Express office. They both got off their horses and walked inside, noticing it had been recently used.

Sarah looked at the Marshal. "Paige, Keith, and two more must have been here," she said, pointing to several fresh tracks. Something in her gut told her to check the bunkhouse. She walked over, following that instinct, and found a note. The message read:

"Jake Rattle Hufford, my love, we are headed to the canyon. That's where Timothy said Cody and Bill were headed. The storm is bad, so they wanted to hurry and leave before losing the trail. Paige is the only one not suspicious of me. Hell, he actually believes I love him. Love, Mary."

Sarah's heart pounded as she ran back to Johnson, thrusting the letter into his hands. "Marshal, read this."

He read it, his face shifting to shock and concern. "That's how they've been following them," he muttered. Then he looked at Sarah. "We need to move now. No telling how many men Jake has besides Andy and Harry."

Sarah and Marshal mounted their horses. As they rode, Sarah turned to him. "Marshal, the war broke Paige and me up. I fell in love with another man—Randy Loft—and he was abusive. Now that I've come back to Gunbarrel, I'm not losing Paige again. He's a good man, Marshal. He was my first love, and I can't bear the thought of losing him." Tears welled in her eyes.

Marshal Johnson placed a firm hand on her shoulder. "You aren't going to lose him, you hear me? But things are different now. You have feelings for him, but he may not have feelings for you. You have to remember that."

Sarah swallowed hard as he continued. "You saw Paige again when you moved back, and I saw the way he looked at you when he was picking up supplies for his mother. I remember that because I'm observant. He didn't just say hi— he talked to you like it was yesterday. But instead of courting, you two just danced around the bush."

Sarah wiped her tears away, realizing he was right. Things might be different, or they might be the same. Either way, she needed to tell Paige how she felt.

She looked at the Marshal. "I'll tell him."

He nodded. "You better," he said with a smile. "Let's ride."

As they made our way through the valley, Marshal Johnson suddenly looked up, his face darkening.

"Comanches," he said under his breath.

Sarah stiffened, following his gaze.

"Don't pull out your gun," he warned. "Stay calm."

More Comanches emerged from behind them. Johnson's grip tightened on the reins. "It's a war party," he muttered. Then, with urgency, he looked at Sarah. "Let's ride like hell!"

They tore through the valley at full speed. The wind ripped Sarah's hat loose, the strap flying behind her. Sarah's pioneer petticoat kicked up dust as their horses thundered forward. The Comanches were closing in, their war cries piercing the air.

Sarah glanced at the Marshal, fear gripping her. "What happens if they catch us?" She shouted.

His face remained grim. "Let's just say it's painful. Either I die first, or you die first. Or we both get captured and tortured. All I know is—we have to keep riding."

Sarah swallowed hard, panic rising in her chest. "Paige better not be dead when we get out of this!" she yelled. "And if we do, his brothers better be alive too! I know I'm supposed to be a lady, but I swear, if I get captured, I might just piss myself!"

The Marshal let out a breath that almost sounded like a laugh, but his tone remained serious. "Keep riding, dammit!" he shouted.

They pushed forward, reaching a steep downslope. They guided their horses down slowly, but the moment they reached the bottom, Sarah and Marshal were surrounded.

Marshal Johnson looked at Sarah. "This is it. You better pray. And don't pull your gun."

Just as a Comanche reached for Sarah, a bugle blast split the air—the U.S. Army Cavalry charge. Texas Rangers, Tonkawas, and other allies stormed in. The Comanches scattered, some falling under gunfire, others fleeing into the hills.

The Marshal and Sarah held their breath, watching the chaos unfold.

Johnson exhaled. "Don't tell my wife, Abigail, we almost got caught by the Comanches. She'll never let me hear the end of it."

One of the cavalry officers, named Bill Roberts, was cocky and eyed Sarah. He spoke to her, "Who might you be, miss?"

Sarah replied with an unpleasant and disgusted tone. "Sarah Calvary."

Marshal Johnson chuckled, knowing that wasn't her last name. He told Bill, "Listen here, Bill, Sarah is married now. Leave her alone."

A Texas Ranger and one of the colonels of the cavalry approached. He whispered to the other, "Leave, or I'll make sure you get punished."

Bill Roberts hesitated but eventually left.

John and the colonel both introduced themselves to Sarah and Marshal Johnson. "I'm Colonel Jerry Garrett, and this is Texas Ranger John Saftler."

Sarah shook both of their hands, and Marshal Johnson did the same. "I'm Marshal Johnson, and this is Sarah Calvery."

Jerry spoke, "Are you married to Paige Calvery?"

Sarah lied but tried not to show it. "Yes, I am," she answered.

John spoke next. "We both served with your husband in the Confederacy."

Marshal Johnson and Sarah were surprised. Sarah asked, "So, you two served with him and Matt together?"

Jerry nodded. "Yes, ma'am. Those two were rough, not afraid of taking orders. They were something—very good men."

John asked, "Where is your husband, and how is he doing, Mrs. Calvery?"

Sarah replied with worry, glancing at Marshal Johnson before speaking. "He is going after his three brothers—Matt, Bill, and Cody. He also has his brother Keith and Mary, who is dangerous to them. And the third is a tracker named Timothy. We've been following them, but we're also tracking three men who framed Matt, Cody, and Bill. Those three men—Jake 'Rattlesnake' Hufford, Harry 'The Bull,' and Andy 'The Hangman' Jackson—have a whole gang."

John looked at Jerry. "You remember that man, Mark Mason? He was telling us about U.S. Army rifles being stolen, whiskey being robbed off whiskey drummers, and women being kidnapped and given to the Comanche."

Jerry Garrett nodded. "Yeah. They call themselves Comancheros. Mark Mason was a gambler, and he was one of their leaders before he turned informant."

Sarah and Marshal Johnson's eyes widened in realization. Johnson spoke up. "Wait a minute. Mark Mason was the gambler who was killed in the saloon in Gunbarrel. Rumors had it that it was over money, and others said it was over a woman—that was the reason Jake killed him."

John looked at Marshal Johnson and Sarah. "Nope, that wasn't the reason at all. If anyone knew the real reason—especially someone in the saloon, like Matt—they would've been killed. Those Comancheros don't mess around. Just think for a minute, Marshal, Sarah—how was Mark killed?"

Sarah answered, "The candles in the saloon blew out because of the wind. It was perfect timing to grab Mark and shoot him in the back."

John looked at them. "The saloon has windows, right? Just a swing door. How is a strong wind going to blow out the candles inside? And if the wind did blow, how would Harry 'Texas Bull' and Andy 'Hangman' Jackson know exactly when to grab him? When the wind would blow? You don't. You distract Mark while he's gambling. How? Mary—she gets all lovey-dovey with the guy. Then, you coordinate. You know Jake has a gang, so you make sure your men are lined up. Then, you give the signal. When the first heavy wind blew, someone blew out the candles."

Sarah frowned. "But the saloon keeper said the wind blew hard."

Jerry spoke up. "Yeah, you're talking about Jerry McDonald."

Marshal Johnson looked at Jerry and John. "How do y'all know?"

John handed him a telegraph. "Two weeks ago, he was arrested for stealing from a whiskey drummer. He confessed, and he was hanged for distributing stolen goods and supplying firearms to the Comanche."

Sarah looked at John. "If Matt, Cody, and Bill were framed, why are they following Paige and Keith? And why is Mary giving them locations?"

Marshal Johnson nodded. "Sarah has a point. I mean, why chase someone you framed, especially when there's no bounty?" His eyes widened as realization dawned on him. "Unless Mark Mason gave one of the brothers some information to hand over to the Texas Rangers personally. Mark knew his time was up. Gambling was his game—he knew how to hand something over without causing a scene. Then, when one of the brothers picked it up and stuck it in his pocket—right before Mark was shot—someone must have seen it. And it had to be Mary. Mary told Jake. Jake told Jerry McDonald. And Jerry told everyone how to do it—the wind and candle trick. That way, no one knew the truth. Matt, Cody, and Bill would be charged with murder instead of just killing them outright."

Sarah shook her head. "They couldn't, because they were too fast. But my question is—who helped them escape so quickly?"

Marshal Johnson looked at Sarah. "It doesn't matter. Paige, Keith, Cody, Bill, and Timothy are in trouble. They have a whole gang after them. We better move now."

Colonel Jerry Garrett turned to some of his men. "You're coming with me."

Captain John Saftler of the Texas Rangers commanded his company. "Move out!"

Marshal Johnson looked at Sarah and smirked. "Looks like we got us some men."

Chapter 5: The Messenger and the Truth

I was sitting at the cabin, cleaning my .45-70 Sharps rifle, right on edge, waiting for Jake and his men. Keith was cleaning his Army Colt .45 revolver. I looked at him.

"Did you clean your .56-50 Spencer rifle?" I asked.

Keith chuckled. "You know I did."

Matt twirled his .45 Dragoon conversion. I heard him ask, "You get yours converted too?"

I chuckled and handed it over. "You know I did."

Bill walked up with his 1866 Henry .44 caliber and his Colt .45 Army revolver. Timothy showed up with his old 1855 Springfield musket, .58 caliber, his double-barrel 12-gauge shotgun, and his 1851 .36 caliber revolver.

I looked at him, impressed. "Damn, you act like the war's still going."

Timothy looked at me. "You got a brain pill?"

I handed him a cigarette. "Where's Cody?"

"Probably cleaning his rifle," Matt said.

Cody sat on a log behind the cabin, reading a note. "There's a shipment of guns heading to Dalesworth. A whole damn shipment. Comancheros are gonna be waiting for it. You gotta hurry."

It was addressed to Texas Ranger John Saftler from Mark Mason.

"P.S. I even got the map. Took it from Jake."

Cody walked over to the group and reached into his cotton sack, pulled out the map, and studied it. He took a deep breath, knowing he had to explain why Jake and his gang wanted the group all dead. Cody remembered Mark Mason handing him the note and the map, telling him to get it to the Rangers—but the only way it would reach them was if Sarah showed up.

I missed Sarah and, without even knowing it, I said out loud, "Sarah, where are you?"

Matt and Bill glanced at each other, then at Cody. Bill whispered, "Paige's gonna be in love... or pissed... or something when Sarah shows up."

Cody looked at them. "She *is* coming alone, right? I mean, she helped us leave town. She told us where this cabin was. The whole damn saloon turned on us. Paige, Keith, and Timothy are here to save our hides—but face it, we're about to go up against a whole gang. We don't have any help... unless Sarah shows."

Matt looked at Cody. "We're getting out of this."

Bill nodded. "Matt's right. And Paige and Keith ain't gonna let us down. Plus, we got Timothy. That's three folks. Add us, that's six."

Matt added, "And don't forget—me and Paige been through worse. Trust me. We were at the Second Battle of

Manassas. We ran, regrouped, and came back to fight again at Palmito Ranch under General Hood."

Bill and Cody stared at him, mouths hanging open. It was the first time they'd heard of a major battle like that. They were used to hearing about smaller skirmishes, not the real bloodbaths.

"Damn, y'all never told us that," Cody said.

I walked in, cigarette in my mouth, and leaned against a tree. Keith and Timothy followed behind me. Timothy looked at me.

"Paige, I got a question for you," he said.

I looked at him. "Yeah?"

"You were at Bull Run?"

I nodded. "Me and Matt. Both of us."

Timothy shook his head and said sarcastically, "Hell of a brutal day, huh?"

Before I could answer, Matt jumped in. "Y'all were brutal with that heavy artillery, blasting us to pieces!"

I looked at them both. "Alright, enough. We need to calm down."

I pulled out a bottle of Dead Eye whiskey, popped the cork, and took a swig. Let it burn a little. Then I handed it to Matt, who passed it to Timothy, then to Bill and Cody.

Cody finally spoke up, voice low. "I know the real reason Mark Mason was killed."

We all looked at him with serious expressions.

Keith asked, "Why?"

"When Mark was playing poker, he handed me this," Cody said, holding up the note and map again. "That woman, Mary, must've seen it and told Jake. There's a shipment of guns heading to Dalesworth. A whole shipment. Comancheros are waiting for it. Mark wrote to Ranger John Saftler and gave me the map. He took it from Jake himself."

I looked at everyone. "So basically, this ain't an ordinary gang. These guys do business with Comanches. And not just that—that's the whole reason you, Cody, Matt, and Bill were all accused. That whole saloon was filled with Comancheros. Instead of killing y'all, they wanted to frame you three. And how in the hell did y'all escape, just outta curiosity?"

Matt, Bill, and Cody looked down, knowing I hated to hear Sarah's name being involved.

Keith, being the oldest of us four, asked with a demanding voice, "Who helped y'all?"

Matt answered, "Sarah Rogers."

I spit out my drink and yelled, "You three farts got her involved?! Y'all do realize Comancheros and Comanches work together, right? And please tell me she didn't say she was coming here."

Matt yelled back, "She insisted! And plus, she told us about this cabin. In fact, she was gonna spread rumors when we left town, saying that Jake and his men were the ones who killed the gambler."

Keith looked at me. "Paige, that's why the Marshal sent you to look for Cody, Bill, and Matt first—because Sarah's the type to help friends in need. Plus, that Sheriff, Charles Ingleton, is too damn lazy to get off his ass and help. He would've accused them and hung them just 'cause a bunch of Comancheros told him to. Marshal Johnson ain't that dumb, you know."

Keith looked at me, Cody, Bill, Matt, and Timothy. "Look, Paige, you and Sarah are both stubborn as hell. And just think—Marshal Johnson knows y'all well. His wife, Abigail Johnson, told him that Mom came to town to keep an eye on all you when y'all were younger—'cause y'all's asses couldn't stay out of trouble."

Matt laughed, remembering. "Remember that time when I snuck out of church, and Paige and Sarah walked in with dirt on their clothes, messy hair, and hay on them? Mom and grandma Charlotte, were pissed, but they decided to tell everyone in church they were trying to catch a loose chicken."

Everyone laughed.

Keith nodded. "Yeah, I remember. I got my buster whipped by Dad and got extra work."

I looked at them. "Yeah, come on, Sarah and I were teenagers. And plus, she was a hellfire."

Keith said, "I'm pretty sure that Sarah and the Marshal are riding together. Sarah's too damn stubborn. And she's a fighter. She may have her moments like a woman, but she can shoot."

I looked at them. "I did see a woman and man riding together a month back, after I killed those bandits. But it was a good mile away, and the sun was so bright."

I turned to Keith. "We're going to face a fight, knowing them sons of bitches are coming back. And that damned woman who used me might fight with them. Meanwhile, we've got a fighting ex-Yankee who's a scout to ex-Rebels, and three regular ranchers who can shoot. Then, if Sarah and the Marshal arrive, that'll be two extra guns—if we're not dead, and if Sarah and the Marshal aren't dead either, cause of the Comanches or bandits. We got lucky we didn't get picked off already."

Keith, Matt, Bill, Cody, and Timothy looked at each other.

"This is some battle we're facing," Timothy said.

I looked at them and said, "We just need to barricade the cabin and get the horses ready to ride out if hell breaks loose— cut and run. I don't know what their attack plan is, and we don't know if they're out there gathering Comanche. All cause that gambler, Mark Mason, gave you, Cody, a tip and didn't tell the Marshal himself. Maybe he was just too damn scared—or maybe it was too obvious."

Matt spoke. "We're just going to have to do what we did in that war, brother." He looked at me, grabbed his rifle, and said, "Give them the hate. Flank them, set up traps, and give them the fight that we gave the Yankees."

I looked at him and remembered the term *Angel Heart*— where the memories and dreams returned, remembering the cruelty. Me and him turned straight-up killers. We didn't show mercy.

I remembered the time we got surrounded by the Yankees. Me and him picked up rifles off the dead, fought, and took the wounded ones, tied them to trees, and cut their throats. When the others came at us on horses, we hit them with the buttstocks of our guns. Then we bayoneted them. When more came, we ran into the woods and hid, then flanked them using cannonballs packed with   gunpowder and nitroglycerin—like TNT. We lit the fuses and threw them. We killed with no mercy.

That was damn near every battle until we had to fall back. We got a nickname that spread: *The Brothers of Death.*

I was shaken.

Matt said, "Hey man, you okay? You look like you're dead standing."

I looked at him. "I'm fine."

Keith looked at me. "You sure?"

I looked at everyone. "Yeah, I'm sure. Let's prepare for battle."

I looked at Timothy. "You go take watch at the front window. Bill, you take watch out the back window. Keith, you take the window on the side."

I turned to Matt. "Me and you take cover at the wagon. I'll take cover at that rocky slope. We should have a strong holding position, 'cause look—there's only two ways in. Both paths are the south and north entrances. They're coming from either direction. The only advantage they have is the cliffs on both sides of us."

Keith kept an eye on the south side, and Bill and Timothy were overseeing the north. Cody and I monitored both cliffs.

'We should have a good vantage point,' I thought.

Cody pulled out his cap and ball pistol with the broken hammer and whispered to himself, "My backup." Then he drew his other revolver and a rifle. Bill had his rifle and revolver ready. Timothy had his rifle, shotgun, and revolver at hand. Keith was ready too.

Suddenly, the back door got kicked in. Cody got shot in the arm. He looked up and saw Harry, and yelled, "They're here!"

Before Harry could fire, Cody's broken revolver fell to the ground and spun once. By pure luck, the hammer hit the ground just right, causing it to fire—striking Harry in the leg. It bought Cody just enough time to shoot him in the chest with his Army Colt .45.

Cody yelled, "I got Harry!"

Bill spotted one of the Comancheros and fired his shot from his 1866 Henry flat golden .44. The bullet hit the rider in the side, sending him flying off his horse.

Keith saw another Comanchero riding in with a torch. He aimed his .56-50 Spencer rifle, and the rimfire cartridge fired as the hammer dropped. The bullet flew straight into the Comanchero's heart.

Meanwhile, Timothy used his shotgun to take down two riders.

Bullets from the Comancheros tore into the cabin, splintering the walls and doors, shattering glass. The smell of dirt and gunpowder triggered memories—me and Matt, back in combat. I shot from the rocky slope with my 1874 Sharps, fast reloading, taking down riders in the distance. My shots found their marks.

Matt fired his .45 Dragoon, then pulled out its twin. He dual-wielded, dropping two more riders off their horses.

Cody tried to bandage his arm, but every time he did, another Comanchero fired at him.

He yelled, "Y'all sons of bitches, let me bandage my arm!"

Timothy yelled back, "It doesn't work that way, Cody!"

Timothy quickly helped wrap the wound while yelling, "Bill, cover us!"

Bill covered them from both windows, taking out more Comancheros with fast reflexes. He reloaded quickly as Timothy finished the bandaging and ran back to watch the north side window.

That was when Jake saw him—and shot him in the chest.

Keith yelled, "Tim's been shot!"

Bill checked and yelled, "He's dead!"

I heard Bill and cursed, "Damn it!" I started to get fiery mad. I pulled out my .44 Dragoon and began firing with fury.

Then I heard a voice yell, "Y'all boys are dead! I'm gonna hang y'all's bodies!"

I recognized it—it was Andy, the Hangman Kid. I watched him walk out from behind me. But I didn't give him the chance. I shot him and sent him falling to his death.

The Comancheros scattered and rode away.

Matt yelled, "They'll be back! Let's get ammo and more weapons!"

Me, Cody, Bill, Keith, and Matt started gathering weapons from the twenty dead Comancheros. That was when I heard hooves pounding the dirt—someone was riding fast toward us.

I looked up and saw Mary riding in hard.

I glanced at Keith, Matt, Cody, and Bill—and chuckled.

They all looked at me.

"What's so funny?" Matt asked.

I shrugged. "Guess she's man-trapping me now that she's a widow."

Keith laughed, but stopped short when Mary rode up, out of breath.

"Comanches and Comancheros—they're coming this way!" she shouted.

I turned to the others. "Let's get in the cabin. Now."

Mary followed us in. She saw Timothy's dead body being dragged by Bill and Cody. Her face filled with worry.

"Oh my God, Cody—you're hurt!"

I looked at her. "Don't say anything, Mary. Not to us. You know what you did."

Mary spoke quietly, "I'm sorry... I do love you."

Keith yelled, "Guys! The Comancheros and Comanches are coming!"

I yelled, "Everyone, take positions! Try not to let them smoke us out!"

I aimed my Sharps rifle and fired.

I looked at everyone. "We shoot all at once—we gotta make every shot count. But be smart. They're going to try and circle around us. That's when we hit 'em."

"They'll pull tricks to try and scare us," I added, "but guess what? Let's show them how us cavalry brothers get brutal."

Matt yelled, "Remember—we just collected guns and belts from twenty bodies. We should be able to hold out."

Mary tried to grab a gun. Bill kicked it away from her.

Mary looked at him, pleading, "Please, let me help. Please—I can shoot!"

I looked at her. "We don't trust you."

Mary begged, tears in her eyes, "I don't want to die... It's only five of you—how do you even think you can manage?"

Cody spoke up, "We've dealt with a lot of bullshit."

Bill said, "Shit, seen so much killing—and you betrayed my brother. You led those men to follow us."

Matt glared at her. "And you played the gambler like a fool... got him murdered."

Chapter 6: The Final Battle

Everyone in that saloon even claimed it to be true hell.

"Hell, me and Paige here fought in one war, and this is the second one for us," I said to Mary. "Mary, you sit down and be quiet, 'cause I'm going to tell you something. A man lost his life because of you. Cody got shot because of you. Your boyfriend got killed because of you. And his friends—and more of his friends—are going to die. You wanna know why? Because of your stupid game, having them follow me, Keith, and Timothy."

There was a rumbling outside, but I was lost in my anger, "How dare-"

Keith interrupted, "I hear the Comanche and Comancheros yelling, laughing, and making noises."

I looked at Keith, Matt, Cody, and Bill. "Let's kill these bastards."

We went to the windows of the cabin. When they circled around us, we each fired, hitting our mark. We took cover and fired again, landing more hits. Keith shot one carrying a torch, not caring whether it was Comanche or Comanchero. Bill shot one off a cliff. Cody hit one trying to launch a flaming arrow. Matt took down one sneaking from the rear. I shot one trying to flank us—but then an arrow struck my shoulder.

I dropped my rifle and broke the arrow. I looked at Keith. He was in shock and was trying to get to me. "Keep shooting, dammit!"

Keith looked at Bill, Cody, and Matt. They kept firing. Mary bandaged my arm as I pulled out my revolver. She was panicking.

"Stay down," I told her as I aimed and kept firing.

I grabbed an extra pistol and fired again. An hour passed.

Matt asked each of us, "How much ammo?"

I looked at him.

"Out. You?"

"I don't have any," he replied. Keith and Bill said the same.

I looked at Mary, knowing what they'd do to her—torture her, scalp her. Then suddenly, just as the Comanche and Comancheros made their final charge, the Texas Rangers, U.S. Cavalry, and Tonkawa warriors charged in.

Matt spoke, "I think that's the Tonkawa, 'cause they're shootin' the Comanche and Comancheros."

Some of the enemy ran; others were killed.

Matt and I heard Marshal Johnson yell, "Boys, y'all can come out now!"

Me, Matt, Bill, Cody, Keith, and Mary walked outside. Mary suddenly grabbed a gun and shouted, "I'm not getting turned in!" She raised it at us.

'This Bitch,' I thought. *'I can't believe she made me fall for her.'*

Sarah quickly shot her before I could.

Matt said, "Damn," then looked at Keith, Bill, and Cody. "We knew she could shoot, but hellfire, that's something."

John Saftler looked at me and Matt. "Never thought I'd see y'all again."

He looked at me. "Your wife," he said, pointing to Sarah.

I looked at Sarah with a smirk, knowing she'd lied about being married to me. Matt, Keith, Bill, and Cody tried not to laugh.

I looked at John. "What'd she do?"

John replied, "Well, your wife's somethin'. Doesn't like being told what to do, and she's mighty protective. But I gotta say—you're a lucky man. And by the way, if you and Matt need a job, Texas Rangers are always needin' help. That is, if you two want it."

Jerry Garret walked up to me and Matt.

"Find a job here, boys. Good seein' y'all again. And no need to explain—we already know what y'all know."

Matt looked at him. "You know you're a galvanized Yankee now?"

I broke out laughing. "Went from blue to gray."

Before Matt could say something else, Sarah jumped in.

"That's not nice! If it weren't for him, my husband Paige, the cavalry could've died!"

She noticed the bandages on me and Cody's arms.

"You two been hurt?"

Garret called for his doctors. One worked on the bullet in Cody's arm, pulling it out. The other drove the arrow forward through my shoulder, then stitched it up. Both doctors said we'd be fine.

I looked at Garret and John.

"Me and Matt want to thank you for savin' our rumps. And it's good seein' y'all both."

They looked at us.

John said, "Hell, y'all were the best in our unit. But we better get goin'. Got a job to do."

Me and Matt waved them goodbye and watched the Texas Rangers, U.S. Army, and Tonkawa ride off. I looked at Marshal Johnson.

"Thanks for keepin' Sarah safe."

Then I looked at Sarah, knowing we had to talk. I looked down at Mary's body, knowing I would never see her again. *'Good Riddance,'* I thought.

I turned to Matt, Keith, Cody, and Bill.

"Can you give me and Sarah a minute?"

Bill replied, "Yeah, you two are married. Need some alone time." They all laughed.

Sarah said, "I shouldn't have told them we were married. I knew your brothers were going to make a mess."

I looked at her. "Why did you?"

With a chuckle, she replied, "'Cause some young lieutenant tried to flirt with me. And you know I'm not just a woman who wants that kind of attention. And plus—"

Before she could finish, Marshal Johnson told Matt, Keith, Bill, and Cody to quit beating around the bush. They nodded, knowing. Keith added, "That woman's been wantin' that boy ever since she came back to Gunbarrel."

Then Sarah looked at me, tears in her eyes. "I can't, Paige."

I looked at her. "What is it? I need to know."

"I need to know if you love me. We've been together since that stupid war. And when you were gone so long, I thought you were dead. Then I got with that damn Randy Loft. He didn't treat me good, and everyone mocked me and shamed me for divorcing him, even though he abused me. That's why I moved back to Gunbarrel. Then I saw you again, and it felt like we were young again."

I couldn't take it anymore. I kissed her lips gently. Pulling away, I said, "I do love you. And I want to be with you. I'm glad you called me your husband—so no woman can go after me."

Sarah chuckled, and we kissed. Keith, Matt, Cody, Bill, and Marshal Johnson all cheered.

Our Ranch

Two Years Later

Under the big oak tree where I had said goodbye to Sarah 13 years earlier before going off to war, we finally stood together again—this time, to be married.

My mother, Betsy, my father, Reno, Sarah's mother, Charolette Mills, her father, Travis Mills, and Keith, Cody, Matt, Bill, Marshal Johnson, and his wife, Abigail, all gathered to watch the pastor wed us.

It was the happiest day of my life.

The End

References

Wikipedia contributors. (n.d.). *Second Battle of Bull Run.* Wikipedia. Retrieved April 17, 2025, from https://en.wikipedia.org/wiki/Second_Battle_of_Bull_Run

Wikipedia contributors. (n.d.). *Texas in the American Civil War*. Wikipedia. Retrieved April 17, 2025, from https://en.wikipedia.org/wiki/Texas_in_the_American_Civil_War

Wikipedia contributors. (n.d.). *Comanchero*. Wikipedia. Retrieved April 17, 2025, from https://en.wikipedia.org/wiki/Comanchero

Legends of America. (n.d.). *Old West slang, lingo & phrases – A writer's guide to the Old West*. Retrieved April 17, 2025, from https://www.legendsofamerica.com/we-slang/

Texas State Historical Association. (n.d.). *Indian tribes of Texas. Texas State Historical Association*. Retrieved April 17, 2025, from https://www.tshaonline.org/handbook/entries/indians-of-texas

Texas Highways. (n.d.). *The original Texans. Texas Highways Magazine*. Retrieved April 17, 2025, from https://www.texashighways.com/culture/the-original-texans/

Special Thanks To My Friends

To,

Matt Baker

Keith Eckermann

Cody Jordan

Bill Jordan

Thank you for assisting me throughout this writing process, providing me with ideas, and most importantly, for allowing me to include you in my book. You have made my story feel so alive.

www.ingramcontent.com/pod-product-compliance
Lightning Source LLC
Chambersburg PA
CBHW040842010826
48978CB00012BB/869